RE: NA

Mark O'Regan

Tuma and his American counterpart O'Brien looked across to one another; months of counter-intelligence were about to come down to these eight men on board the SH60SEA hawk en route to a container ship carrying a nuclear bomb 40 miles off the coast of Tuma's native New Zealand. The order had been given to neutralise the threat before the Rena arrived at its final destination, Auckland. Auckland is New Zealand's largest city and is about to hold its largest international event, the Rugby World Cup final, which will be above an estimated global audience of 2 billion.

His new friend O'Brien had fought with Tuma before in the mission to prevent one of the cleanest environments on the planet from being a radioactive wasteland. Only three buildings in the developed world were aware of the magnitude of what was happening: The White House, The Pentagon, and the US Embassy in Wellington, which had the Prime Minister of New Zealand and the Defence Minister of New Zealand.

Tuma was a former New Zealand SAS seasoned pro, but his country, although renowned for their skill level and bravery, did not have anything remotely like the sophistication and technology of the seals. The red light came on, signalling the drop zone was 30 seconds away;

O'Brien reached over and checked Tuma's kit and gave him a nod and smile. The Black Hawke dropped the inflatable first, then, like the well-oiled aching seals, they stood off chopper foot, one by one, and dropped into the wintery waters of the South Pacific, 5km from the target.

The icy cold water helped Tuma clear his mind and focus on the others. This might be a highly important operation, but for him, it was his birthplace, his whanau (family), and his friends. It was everything he loved, and failure was not an option. He held up his arm, and O'Brien lifted it as he slipped over the edge and into the inflatable last.

Everyone had removed their masks and had night vision on as they sped toward the stern of the 236-meter container ship. Except for the seal team commander who was steering the inflatable towards the dim light aboard the Rena, everyman was double-checking his M4A1 carbine, checking spare mags. Tumu put his hand on the loaded M11 Sig Saver P228, which comforted him, knowing how accurate and reliable they were. Each man carried a special backpack with radiation protection kits so they could disarm the nuke once the terrorists were neutralised.

The Rena was still moving at the maximum speed of 21knots; the little inflatable was getting thrown around by the wash from the Rena's massive 3351 tonne, and every man was holding on as tight as they could. Seals No. 2 grabbed a device Tuma had only ever seen the day before as it was a highly classified device; the commander steered the inflatable expertly within a meter of the massive ship. The device roared as the gas cartridge exploded, sending a grappling hook 23 meters above, which clambered over the rail. Tuma looked on in admiration of the skill and balance of the navy seal as he clicked the winch, and 23 meters of steel ladder slid up the side of the container ship. Seaspray was making visibility incredibly difficult. O'Brien was to be the first up, followed by Tuma and then the other six seals. The Seal Team leader put the 10-second timer on to cut the inflatable motor, leaving it to be picked up later by the crew on The USS John Paul Jones.

Once all on board the Rena, the eight men split into four teams of 2; Tuma and O'Brien were to take control of the bridge, the Seal commander and the bomb specialist were tasked with locating and deactivating the bomb, while the other four men were to neutralise the terrorists and keep non-combatants in a safe, contained place and cable tied for their and the safety of the mission.

Mission Control was directing all the operatives to go; securing the top deck was first as they split into four going down the port and 4 taking starboard. Tuma had never had satellite directions before, but he instantly recognised the advantage it gave over other special forces teams like the New Zealand SAS he had been part of. The seal commander led the way, followed by O'Brien, and then Tuma and the bomb specialist covered the rear. With the target at 20 meters, the headpiece chirped; this is where it was going to get tricky. If they held a gun, they would be executed. If not, they had to be taken quietly, gagged, and bound.

The commander held his hand up for the other three men to pause; he signalled O'Brien forward. Two men were smoking cigarettes and laughing at some unheard joke, seemingly without a care in the world. There was no way to approach them; it was exactly the situation everyone didn't want. Are they terrorists or not? O'Brien said through the coms, "Let's get Tuma to bang one of the containers so they can hear, and let's see how they react." The seal commander nodded, and Tuma went behind the closest container, which was 25 feet from the men, and banged the butt of his M4AI onto the container three times as hard as he could. The men stopped laughing, dropped their cigarettes, reached down, and picked up guns. They died in 0.8 of a second after they became visible to the seal leader and O'Brien. "Two armed bogies down," the seal leader said into the mic, simultaneously notifying the other four seals and the command ops that there were armed men on the deck of the container ship, signifying that the intel was correct and the mission was live.

The Prime Minister of New Zealand, a small South Pacific nation, looked out the window of his security-detailed vehicle as he sped through the streets of Wellington on his way to the American Embassy. Beside him were the heads of New Zealand's Defence Force and the Intelligence Service, The SIS. Globally, New Zealand has the 52nd largest economy in the world; the island nation makes 240 billion annually, most of that from primary agriculture, fishing, and tourism, with a population of 5 million. Historically, New Zealand, along with close neighbours Australia, the United States of America, and Canada, are mostly populated by refugees searching for a better life from the United Kingdom.

Having been a highly successful banker for Merrill Lynch in New York, the Prime Minister knew firsthand that most Americans would not even know where New Zealand was, what they did, or even that they had distant relations there as the late President Ronald Reagan did. New Zealand had contributed a lot per capita to the wars and had a strong military alliance with The United States and Australia known as ANZUS, that was until the country declared itself Nuclear-free in 1987. The policy required deflation of whether ships entering its waters carried nuclear weapons or not. Of course, this, strategically and militarily, was not a concession that the mighty United States would agree to, especially given that the country was equivalent in population to South Carolina.

From that point in time, especially under Republican Presidents, trade and defence support had been affected. New Zealand has an exclusive economic zone of over 4 million square kilometres with a navy consisting of 9 vessels and an Air Force with 48 aircraft, none of which are fighter jets. Actually, protecting that amount of area was next to impossible. With an army of 15000, the truth of the matter was that New Zealand was economically and militarily a small fish in the context of the globe.

The American Embassy destination took the Prime Minister's vehicle through the skirts of Wellington's famed bars and clubs district, Courtney Place. The clubs and streets looked full as patrons sprawled out looking for taxis home as the entertainment venues cashed in on the Rugby World Cup tourists from the 20 countries participating in the world's 3rd largest sporting event. The irony of New Zealand being the big fish of a tournament that had teams from The United States and Russia, who in rugby prowess were the small fish.

The New Zealand Prime Minister had been to the US Embassy before, but the security was visibly different this time. As the Prime Minister, Defence Minister, and Intelligence Chief made their way to the US Embassy's 'Secure Communications Room,' they were all in awe of the sophistication and gadgetry visible. The US Embassy, normally a chirpy diplomat, was incredibly somber and serious as he shook each of the 3's hands and motioned for each to take their seat, directing the Prime Minister to the head of the table. Two screens immediately came to life; one looked like the inside of a helicopter with night vision, and the other held the face of The United States of America's President and a dozen men in uniform. "Good morning, John and gentlemen."

Potus Obama flashed a brief smile, and all three gentlemen responded with "Good morning, Mr President."

"Gentleman, we have located the device, thanks to some great intel from O'Brien and your man Manu. In recognition of the great work from these two, I gave permission for them to be on the chopper with Seal Team 5, which you can see on the other screen". "Prime Minister, as I briefed you at our golf game in Hawaii, our intelligence people had picked up chatter regarding a 'Huge Blow' against Satan and his minions at a significant event in the South Pacific."

"Apologies for having to bring you in at our Embassy, but the encryption we are using is highly advanced, and we do not share it with any ally country."

The three men nodded in, acknowledging the sensitivity of it all. "John, our eight men are on route to a container ship 40 miles off the coast of Tauranga; we believe it has ten members of a Chechen terrorist group that arose from the ashes of the second Russian/Chechen war, which started in 1999 and was ended two years ago. Prime Minister, the Russians were extremely brutal to the Chechens in this war. Our estimates were over 80,000 were killed, including women and children. It's just a fact, a gentleman, when you cause that much pain and suffering to a people, you directly spawn and give all the nurturing to equal amounts of evil."

A third screen lit up, "Gentlemen, this is Asma Eliiza; his father was the leader of the Islamic Separates who tried to take control of the backed Chechen Government. His father was brutally executed in the Chechen capital, and Eliiza has sworn revenge on Russia and the West as the Wet couldn't/wouldn't help. I personally think we made a mistake; it is my personal opinion this was only the start of President Putin's 1st. I believe he has ambitions to retake all the former USSR. But my former European counterparts are seemingly under Putin's spell; something doesn't ring true about him. Unfortunately, where this affects you is that he will be in Auckland on his super yacht to rendezvous with one of his closest oligarchs, who is a rugby fanatic and will be moved to Auckland Harbour for the next three weeks."

"Apologies for being so brief, gentlemen, but the operation is about to go live. John, we have all the chefs of the staff here. John, this is your country. I am appointing you commander and chief for the next hour. We will all advise you, but ultimately, you will have control of our Seal Team and what they do. I'll pass you now to Major General Micheals to brief you on the nuclear device."

"Gentlemen, we are dealing with a former Soviet block nuclear device; it's the equivalent of 0.3 kilotons. If detonated, it would produce a fireball, shockwaves, and deadly radiation to everything within a 10-kilometre radius. It would be a 100% fatality rate. 10 to 50 kilometres, 25% would die of cancer within 12 months. All agriculture, fishing, and soil would be contaminated for 200 years". The Prime Minister of New Zealand's face went noticeably pale. "It's ok," Potus Obama said. "Welcome to my world."

Tuma held his young nephew back; his dog had chased a pig into Bund Mans Canyon; listen, nephew, there is no way out of there; see how my dogs are waiting out here in the clear? In another 10 seconds, that pig is going to realise it's cornered and is going to spin straight around and carry on running back this way fucking fast and angry, so get ready and remember a little Prayer for the pig. Wait till the dogs tire it, I'll say when, but go lift up its front left leg, slide the knife straight in, and cut down. Cut the arteries, and it will bleed out quickly, so less suffering for the pig, which means better meat for us Kapai? Yes, Uncle.

Right on cue, Tuma's nephew cried, letting out a yelp as the pig came hoofing it through the scrub into the clearing. For a brief second, Tuma saw something like recognition in the pig's eyes, as if it knew it had just fallen into a trap. Tuma and his whanau had been setting for pigs for hundreds of years.

Tuma's dogs worked as one distracted the other two tried to bite the 140-lb boar nuts or legs. There's nothing quite like the shrikes of a pig when it's in danger; its piercing silenced only after it lost enough blood to slip into unconsciousness and die. After tying the legs together to make a backpack out of the pig, Tuma helped, slipped it over his nephew's back, blood all over him and a huge smile; the whanau would heap praise on the young man tonight. A pig this size will yield 30Kgs of meat, plus the bones for boiling up. For a 12-year-old kid to provide that for the whanau was a step towards manhood; while most city 12-year-olds will be wanting iPhones and Nikes rather than providing for their families, they are from them.

Under Tuma's careful instruction, his nephew singed the hair off the pig and gutted it; as they were lifting it up onto the hook, Tuma's ear turned toward the west as he heard the sound of an NH90 helicopter nephew, "fuck off inside and tell your Auntie I'm going up the top paddock to see some old workmates, she will know."

Tuma hopped on his quad and sped up to the top paddock where he knew the chopper would land; his old platoon sergeant from the New Zealand SAS jumped down with a tall pakeha in civilian clothes. The sergeant looked into the cockpit, motioning the chopper to switch off. "Atur Blue," the sergeant said. This was Tuma's nickname as he was half Maori and half Pakeha with blue eyes. "Hey Serg" Tuma said. "What the fuck are you doing here?" There's a situation, and we need you bro

Tumatauenga Thornton Manu was half Naati Porou and half Irish Viking. Tuma was from a small east coast village in New Zealand, Tolaga Bay. Tuma's grandparents had met fighting at Alamein during World War 2. His father in the 28th Battalion, which is New Zealand's most decorated army unit, created such a reputation that Germaine's General Rommel said, "Give me a Maori battalion, and I will conquer the world." His mother's family fought along in the 22nd Battalion.

Against the wishes of his parents and grandparents, Tuma followed his grandfather's footsteps into the New Zealand Army and quickly gained entry into New Zealand's elite SAS. Who, despite not having the technology of other special forces units, had a very good reputation. After having served in overseas deployments to The Balkans and Iraq, Tuma looked set for a high-ranking career in his country's military until the New Zealand Police raids on the Uruwearas, where a lot of his father's whanau lived. The raids were based on the same amount of facts as weapons of mass destruction, which was the basis for the 2003 Iraq invasion.

Tuma walked away from his military career in protest of the unjustified treatment of his whanau. That was in 2007; four years ago, he had not seen his platoon sergeant since then. Tuma looked across to the tall pakeha. The operators knew one another at a glance, and it was like seeing a kindred spirit. Tuma looked at the man and said, "Seal?"

"Yes," the man said, putting out his hand, "Zac O'Brien." Tuma looked back at his serg. Whatever it was, I was not interested. This is bad, Tuma. It is about as bad as it gets; we have a credible threat that there will be a devastating attack at the Rugby World Cup final in Auckland next month. "Oh fucking bullshit, you cunts pulled that shit in Iraq, no-one is going to attack us, fuck half the world doesn't even know we exist."

"That may be true," said O'Brien, "But next month, your country is hosting the 3rd largest sporting event in the world, and unbeknown to almost everyone, the Russian President and his filthy rich mates are going to be there on their super yacht and this crazy Chechen mother fucker will turn your country into Hiroshima just to get revenge on that little Russian prick". Tuma took the file and opened it Andre Petron aka 'Asma Elliza' O'Brien said "so this guys father was the Chechen Rebal Leader who, when the Ruskies eventually won was beheaded live on Chechen TV as a warning to anyone who thought of starting a third Chechen rebellion."

"Petron, aka Asma, was smuggled inside Russia to be a deep cover agent from her early teens. This guys did it all in the Russian Military; he was one of the very best spet snaz, then rose high in the military intelligence. Two months ago, he slipped out of Russia with a 200kg nuclear device with a 0.3 kiloton payload, enough to kill everything within a 30 km radius. He's not after you, Kiwis. You will be collateral damage; he wants Putin. Putin ordered the slaying of his father."

"We don't know where the fucker is. We know he made it out of Europe with the nuclear device; the only chatter our intel people have been able to get is that Rugby World Cup is 'venue' and the 'code sign' is RE: NA."

"Ok," Tuma said, "You got me listening. What do you need me for?" The Sergeant took back over the brief, "We believe he has sucked some gangs here in New Zealand, thinking they are helping smuggle in heroin from Afghanistan. Yes, he will have some for them, but ultimately, he will be smuggling in a nuke which could make their hooch plants florescent for the next 50 years."

Tuma straight away knew where this was headed; like most Maori, the New Zealand government's oppression of all things Maori in the '60s and '70s had driven a lot of whanau into gangs and crime to try and feed and protect their families. Tuma didn't have any gang members on his mother's side, but his dad's side was pretty much every different gang in New Zealand. "Ok," Tuma said, what's the angle?" The Sergeant said, "We want you to act as a go-between for O'Brien, who is a large 'cocaine dealer' whom you knew from Iraq, and you are helping your mate and making a little something on the side for yourself."

Tuma burst out laughing, "No disrespect O'Brien, those gangster mother fuckers will spot you for a pig straight away, and you'll get us both fucking shallow graves." Both men started to talk, and Tuma held up his hand, "Listen, you don't understand how clever and ruthless my people are, O'Brien. You've fucked up already coming here in your chopper, so get back in and fuck off. Let me think about it, but let me tell you this: O'Brien, Rommel didn't say, "Give me a battalion of Americans, and will conquer the world," he said it about us Maori. So listen here, you want to play the part of a big-time dealer, you better be able to handle copious amounts of piss and smoke heaps of weed, you better have a shit load of high-end cocaine, and you better be able to fuck like a rattlesnake, cause they will test you every fucking which way so before we talk about how clever you are, you and I are going to have a big night so I can test you every way myself, except for the fucking part, which will happen, they will send one of their wahines your way to suck your balls dry and see if she can spot a hole in your cover. So I don't give a fuck if you married or not. You will have to screw her, comprendy?"

Both men nodded. The sergeant turned to the pilot and motioned to start it up. He ran to the chopper and came back with a satellite phone, passing it to Tuma, "Our numbers are in it." Tuma looked at O'Brien. "I'll meet you in Hamilton in two days. Have cash and cocaine; I'll bring the buds."

"So you're going to do it?" The sergeant asked. "I'm going to fight for my fucking people and country. I'm just not sure if he can?" Tuma said, pointing at O'Brien.

Andre Petron, due to his reputation and FSB rank, had found the task of taking the 200 0.3 Kiloton nuclear bomb out of a high-security storage area relatively easy; he had, over the last 20 years, strategically placed Chechen loyalists in key roles. He knew firsthand that, like the limited states, all Russian ports had state-of-the-art nuclear radiation detectors. From the nuke onto a helicopter that flew at low altitude to a small Russian airport; it was loaded onto a private cargo plane, which then dropped by parachute into the black sea, where Andre's best hand-picked team had retrieved it onto their sailing yacht as the Russian army was not aware of the missing yacht, Patron was able to go ahead of the yacht as it left the Black Sea flash his credentials and within 24 hours the yacht was off the coast of Athens.

From now on, Andre Patron no longer exists. He could, after 22 years, resume his true identity of Asma Eliza, although, for the next part of the mission, he and his men were part of the Ukauman mafia smuggling 2000 kg of Heroin onboard a Greek registered container ship into New Zealand. It was the signal Asma sent to his father's brother in Chechenia 'RE:NA Satan Glow' that both the NSA and Russian intelligence picked up that not only sent joyous hope throughout Chechenia but alerted both intelligence agencies something was wrong. Within 24 hours, the Russian Military knew they had a small nuclear device missing as well as a high-ranking former Spetzmaz FSB Agent. The intelligence agencies of Russia and America had a secret pact to inform one another of nuclear devices unaccounted for, so every asset of both formidable historic foes was taken with locating it. Asma had planned everything meticulously from the moment he had heard Putin was to attend a sporting event in a small country in the South Pacific with a coastline far too large for their tiny Military to cover, let alone protect. New Zealand had participated in the Infidel War in Afghanistan, so they needed punishment themselves.

The best way to smuggle anything was through the already estimated drug smuggling routes. As far as the stupid, fat Greek Captain of the container ship knew, he was getting 2 million cash to help smuggle heroin into a country, something he had done many times before. What he didn't know was that Asma had made sure that he would also have x-ray machines and tanning beds for New Zealand, which emit radiation so as to give reason for gamma rays if radiation detectors picked up higher gamma rays. The captain of the ship was easily manipulated by women and some of Asma's heroin, so getting a lockable room near the engines of the ship was easy. From here, Asma disconnected the bomb trigger and had his men encase the device in lead glass; he would only need 2 hours to dismantle the casing, insert the trigger, set the timer, and then get at least 50 km away.

Tuma walked into the Ibis Motel in Hamilton, and O'Brien closed the door. Behind him on the table was 10 kg of high-grade cocaine, 100k in cash, two clock pistols, and 100 rounds. Tuma looked at O'Brien and nodded his approval. So far, it's a good seal. For the next 3 hours, Tuma talked through how they would need to get rapid entry into the 'Kingpin World' of the New Zealand drug market to find someone who could give them intel on any

Russian or Eastern European players who were trying to enter the scene. "Right," Tuma said, "I'm going to say a karakia. I'm going to ask IO and all my ancestors to protect us, forgive what we are going to have to do, and guide us to protect our sacred whenuia from such evil" "E Rangi e papa e Te whanau tua whakatohia to koutou manaakitanga ki rotu itenei mahio matuu sky father and earth mother and the family of gods infuse your blessings up this work."

Tuma opened one of the five bottles of 100 Jack Daniels he had brought, "Rack some lines up; from now till we neutralise these fucking terrorists, we are disgruntled ex-military bad arses who are out to make a quick earn and will fuck anyone up who gets in our way." For the next 24 hours, Tuma and O'Brien shared stories from their unique special forces missions and training. The pain, comradely, deaths, and near-death experiences, combined with Jack Daniels and cocaine, bonded the men as only elite operators would know.

Tuma had been a recluse since leaving the SAS and had lived a quiet life with his wife in the isolated East Coast town. Apart from seeing his gangster whanau at Tangis, he had little contact with them. But both men knew that dirty girls were the spies for the gangsters, and so the call went out for 5 of them to party with them in the room. After tipping the girls five grand and having an orgie with them all, with lines of coke, joints, and copious bourbons. A bag of cocaine was strategically left out for one of the women to see. "Hey babe," one of the women said to Tuma, "I've got a friend who would be keen to buy some of that."

For the next 20 days, Tuma and O'Brien gradually worked their way up the pecking order of the gangs in New Zealand, searching for someone who would know of any heroin quantities for trade. After countless lines, drinks, and joints, they set them up with a deal in Tauranga in early October. Tuma's former platoon sergeant, who was their liaison for security intelligence services of New Zealand, who were working with their American counterparts to determine where the Chechens were with their nuke, walked into their motel room which stunk of weed and perfume, had empty bottles of bourbon scattered around "Holly fuck gentleman you took a look like shit!"

Tuma looked at his former boss and said, "Yeah, well, we have checked out vessels coming into Tauranga, and you dumb fucks thought RE:NA meant they would come in through Napier, well RE:NA is actually Rena, a Greek registered container ship arriving tonight!" "Holly fuck!" The sergeant said, "Great work, I've got to go." Tuma and O'Brien both said, "We are going with you. We're going to be on the intercept mission!" The Sergeant knew Tuma well, "Ok, but for fucks sake, get some sleep and clean up; if my boss sees the pair of you right now, you will have no chance!"

The Prime Minister of New Zealand looked on at the live footage of the Seal Team as they killed or bound men aboard the Rena; he had not signed up for this, and watching men die live is not something anyone sane would want to see. Tuma and O'Brien had made it to the bridge and found the Captain and first mate both drunk and wasted. They now had command of this vessel; it would not make it to port now. Unmuffled gunfire rang out in their comms. The terrorists were now alerted to their presence.

Asma woke up to the sound of gunfire. Instantly, he got up and started running towards the engine rooms; if his mission was to fail, who would detonate the nuke and make a statement to the world for letting his Chechen people suffer under the hands of Russia?

The Seal Team Leader said over comms, "Ships secured, no sign of Petron." O'Brien said to the Captain, "You are smuggling a terrorist with a nuclear device on this ship." The Captain's opiate-tinged eyes bulged, "No, no, I wouldn't do that. He only had heroin," as if that was acceptable. "Where is he?" O'Brien said, "He must be in his room, on the engine room deck." "Can we get into it?" O'Brien asked. "There's no way; it's 10 inches of steel," the Captain said. "Show me the blueprints," O'Brien commanded

The Prime Minister and the President both looked at where the room was. "John, my people tell me it'll take 60 minutes to arm the device. I'm going to confide in you that we have a submarine in the area. We can sink that ship now if you give me the order." John's eyes bulged as he looked at the Defence Minister. "They have a submarine in our waters."

"Focus, John. If we torpedo that part of the ship, we can stop him from arming the nuke and contaminating your waters!"

"But how would I explain a nuclear submarine of an ally in our waters?" Key said. Tuma had been studying the charts; he had dived many times here for kiamoana and

23

knew the waters well. "John, there is another option; we are 6 Kilometres from the astrolabe reef; the room he is in is on the starboard bow; the reef would tear the part of the ship open like a tin can!"   Everyone looked and waited for The Prime Minister. He looked at his Defence Minister and Intelligence Chief, and they both nodded. The Prime Minister of the small, very unpopulated island nation gave the order to crash the ship into the reef rather than have a nuclear device detonate or have a nuclear-powered submarine torpedo a vessel in New Zealand waters.